For my sistras, Blue and Fee,

two of my dearest friends – E.A.

For Nathan and Charlotte x – M.B.

First published in 2021 by Scholastic Children's Books
Euston House, 24 Eversholt Street, London NW1 1DB
a division of Scholastic Ltd
www.scholastic.co.uk

London – New York – Toronto – Sydney – Auckland
Mexico City – New Delhi – Hong Kong

Text copyright © Emma Adams, 2021
Illustrations copyright © Mike Byrne, 2021

HB ISBN 978 0702 30766 9
PB ISBN 978 0702 30391 3

The moral rights of Emma Adams and
Mike Byrne have been asserted.

Papers used by Scholastic Children's Books are made
from wood grown in sustainable forests and other controlled sources.

EMMA ADAMS   MiKE BYRNE

UNiCORNS DON'T LOVE RAiNBOWS

■SCHOLASTIC

So many unicorns love to be **happy**,
they spend their days **smiling**
– well I think that's **sappy**.

Yes I **am** a unicorn but
(as you'll see)
there really is something
quite **different**
about me.

Because . . .

I do not like smiling,

I do not like cake,

I do not like ice cream
(makes my
tummy ache).

I **stomp** over rainbows

and will **not** say "WHOOP!"

(and **don't** talk to me about unicorn poop).

My unicorn friends love to **gallop** through flowers,

then lie making daisy chains (literally for hours).

They brew petal perfume,
"DELIGHTFUL!"
they cry

(when I have a sniff, something gets in my eye).

They all **love** bright colours – **especially** pink,
but this in particular makes my heart sink.

For, I have a style that most unicorns lack,
and that is cos my favourite colour is ...

. . . black!

I love black on **everything** and **everywhere**,
my clothes and my bedroom – it's **all** black in there!

If I'm wearing black, then I **never** feel grey,
but when my friends see me . . . they all run away.

Because . . .

My friends **love** rainbows –
they **love** every colour

(but they **don't** love black
cos it makes them feel duller).

They paint rainbow paintings and say it's the norm,
but when I paint mine . . .

"What IS it?"

". . . It's a storm."

Also . . .

They love the sun, but I love when it's pouring – thunder and lightning? That never gets boring!

They **love** karaoke

and I love that too,

but the songs that I like
aren't the ones that they do.

And when it gets dark,
when the day turns to night,

they go to bed early
– well, that's just **not** right!

They **glitter** and **sparkle**,
from heads to their toes

but glitter's **SO** itchy
– as everyone knows.

Suddenly, I realise with a **puff**,
we think differently about all sorts of stuff.

Should I only have friends who think like I do?

Who only like black
(and who hate rainbow poo)?

No!

I can be **me**, and **you** can be **you** –

and we can help others to feel that way too.

For, here is the most helpful thing you will find,

the best thing in life is to **always** be kind.

So if you want a friend, you won't have to go far, and people will **love you** the way that you are.

Remember: your friends can be quite unlike you,
so we **can** be different . . .
and **similar** too!